A BOOK OF DRAGONS

Compiled by Joan Cass

Illustrated by David McKee

BEAVER BOOKS

A Beaver Book
Published by Arrow Books Limited
62-5 Chandos Place, London WC2N 4NW
An imprint of Century Hutchinson Ltd

London Melbourne Sydney Auckland
Johannesburg and agencies throughout the world

First published by Kaye & Ward 1985

Beaver edition 1988
Reprinted 1989 (twice)

Typography and general arrangement
© Kaye & Ward Ltd 1985
Illustrations © David McKee 1985 and 1988

Made and printed in Great Britain by
The Guernsey Press Co. Ltd,
Guernsey, C.I.

ISBN 0 09 954830 5

Contents

To Betty and Peter Swabey
and their grandchildren
with love.

The publishers have made every effort to trace
copyright owners and are grateful to the following
for permission to use copyright material in the
English edition of his book. Penguin Books for *So Big*
from SONGS FOR MY DOG AND OTHER PEOPLE by
Max Fatchen, copyright © 1980 Max Fatchen and
Dragon Fairy from GREEN SMOKE by Rosemary
Manning copyright © 1957 Rosemary Manning;
Irene Elmer for MANDRAGORA'S DRAGON © 1964
Irene Elmer; William Heinemann for *The Snitterjipe*
from PREFABULOUS ANIMILIES by James Reeves;
Blackie & Son Ltd for *Albert's Christmas Party* from
ALBERT AND THE DRAGON by Rosemary Weir and
for THE MAGICIAN AND THE DRAGON by David
McKee; Andre Deutsch for *The Tale of Custard the
Dragon* from I WOULDN'T HAVE MISSED IT by Ogden
Nash.

St. George and the Dragon

At one time in our history England was divided into a number of different kingdoms.

There was, in the North, a knight called Sir George who wanted to escape from court life and travel the world. So he painted a red cross on his shield to show he was a Christian and rode away.

He tried to help the people he met on the road in every way he could.

One evening he came to a small village. Everything was very quiet and as Sir George finished his supper at the village inn he wondered why this was so.

Next morning as he was about to ride away to the nearby town he asked the innkeeper's wife why the inn was deserted and the village so quiet.

The innkeeper's wife wept and told Sir George that the village and town were under a curse.

A dragon who had been sleeping for centuries underground had woken when someone jokingly uttered a magic spell which roused him from his long sleep.

The dragon devoured their crops and animals and then demanded the sacrifice every month of a young boy and girl. Lots were drawn by the people to see whose turn it was next.

Sir George galloped off towards the town where he

discovered the next victim was to be the beautiful daughter of the King himself.

Sir George demanded to be taken to the King who was overwhelmed with grief for his daughter who was bound to a stake at the top of the hill waiting for the dragon to devour her.

Sir George determined to save her and galloped to the top of the hill, drawing his trusty sword.

The dragon suddenly appeared roaring in rage and anger, but Sir George leapt at the beast and slashed him with two mighty strokes in the form of a cross round

his throat. The dragon collapsed panting and exhausted and Sir George led the monster and the princess back to the palace.

The king was overjoyed and offered Sir George money and fame, but he refused. Instead he asked the King, when he had slain the dragon so that it could do no more harm, to become a Christian and cherish and care for the poor of his kingdom.

Then Sir George rode away. Many years after Sir George had become famous for his courage and good works and when he finally died for his beliefs he was known as Saint George. He became the Patron Saint of England and the broad red cross of Saint George now appears on every Union Jack.

Retold by Joan Cass

Bobo

Bobo was a dragon. Most dragons are given names like White Flare or Branduthlon or Proud One or Grinscaling, so Bobo was an unusual name for a dragon but Bobo was an unusual dragon. For one thing he wasn't the same colour all over, his head and claws were dragon green but from his head to his middle was striped blue and white and the rest of him was dark blue. And Bobo didn't breathe fire, never; not even after double strength peppermints. He didn't puff smoke either, not even on a frosty morning.

11

The other dragons were always making fun of him. 'Go back to your ship, sailor,' they'd laugh.

The other dragons were ordinary dragons, big and strong and frightened of nothing, breathing smoke and fire, and they knew they just had to look fierce to get anything they wanted. If a dragon was hungry, he'd go off to a nearby castle or town and kidnap a princess, or, if the princesses were on holiday, a beautiful maiden. If he didn't see a beautiful maiden he'd take any girl.

The dragons wouldn't eat the girls of course. There are much tastier things than girls to eat. No, they'd simply say, 'Give me forty hamburgers, two dozen sausage rolls, five strawberry tarts, twenty doughnuts, a chocolate cake and an apple,' – they always finish with an apple – they think it cleans the teeth. 'If you don't bring me all this,' the dragon would shout, 'I'm going to eat the princess, or beautiful maiden or girl.'

Then the people in the town would get very worried and quickly bring the food. Actually the dragon often worried as well. They worried that one day someone would say, 'Eat her, she's just a trouble-maker, always moaning.' But as far as I know it always worked out all right; the dragon got the food and the girl was freed. Bobo couldn't get his meals in this way because nobody was afraid of him. Instead he had to eat fruit from the trees or rely on snacks that travellers threw to him.

Now all dragons have an incredible craving for ice-cream. When they are very young they eat all they can get but it isn't long before they start to breathe fire and the ice-cream starts to melt, before they can get close enough to even get one lick. Now as Bobo didn't breathe fire, ice-cream was still his favourite food. He'd eat cornets, lollies or choc ices. He wasn't fussy. But ice-cream doesn't grow on trees and passers-by didn't throw it out to him.

Well one day when the sun was high and the birds were at full twitter the dragons were lying about and because they had nothing better to do, (dragons don't read a lot) they were teasing Bobo worse then ever. 'Try eating a box of matches and painting yourself green Bobo,' or 'It's a good job you don't breathe fire, people might think you were a dragon,' or 'You still look like a sailor, why don't you go back to sea?'

Finally Bobo thought: 'I will go to the sea. At least it will be more pleasant than it is here.'

Bobo knew the direction of the sea. He'd watched the sea-gulls come and go and he set off without even bothering to say goodbye. When Bobo saw the sea, it was for the first time in his life. The water was so blue and the sand so gold and the people on the sand looked happy and that made Bobo feel happy too. Then he remembered what a failure he was as a dragon and he decided it might be rather nice to sit down and have a good cry.

He climbed the rocks and found a really uncomfortable place to sit so that it would be easier to cry, and was just settling down when he heard a sobbing sound.

13

The first thing he did was to look at his reflection in a pool to see if he was crying. 'Well, it's not me,' he thought. 'So who is it?' There was another sob and it seemed to come from the other side of the rocks. Bobo peeped over the top. On the other side sat a girl crying into her hanky.

14

'Oh dear, don't cry,' said Bobo. 'I know just how you feel; you're sad because you're not green all over and you can't breathe fire.'

The girl stopped crying and looked up. 'Green all over? Breathe fire? What are you talking about?' she

sniffed. 'Who on earth would want to be green all over and breathe fire?'

'Well, I would,' said Bobo. 'That's why I'm so sad because I'm a funny kind of dragon.'

'You're better off as you are,' said the girl. 'I wouldn't be here talking to you if you breathed fire.'

'I never thought of that,' said Bobo, cheering up. 'My name's Bobo. What's yours?'

'Kate,' sighed the girl, 'and I'm useless. My father makes ice-cream and I'm supposed to sell it, but nobody takes me seriously. I'm so small they go to the other ice-cream sellers and . . .' and she stopped to stare at Bobo. 'What is the matter?' she asked.

Bobo's eyes were getting wider and wider and his tongue was starting to drool. 'Did . . . you . . . say . . . ice-cream?' he stuttered.

'Yes,' said Kate cautiously.

'Oooooh!' groaned Bobo and he closed his eyes and groaned again. 'Oooooh! ice-cream. I'd do anything for ice-cream. Oooooh!'

'Anything?' said Kate excitedly. 'Anything?'

'Anything,' moaned Bobo.

'Would you help me sell ice-creams?' asked Kate.

'Sell ice-creams, me, Bobo, sell ice-creams. Could I shout "Get your lovely ice-creams here"?'

Kate jumped down and from just behind the rock, pushed out her ice-cream cart and gave Bobo a vanilla ice-cream. Bobo's eyes nearly popped out. He sniffed it and gently licked it and then he closed his eyes and ate it as slowly as possible to make it last a long, long time

Then he sighed a great sigh and said, 'That was the best ice-cream in the world.' Kate laughed. 'Have a strawberry one and then you can help me to sell some.'

She had hardly finished speaking when Bobo was off, marching across the sand, pushing the ice-cream cart and shouting, 'ICE-CREAM, LOVELY ICE-CREAM! Come and buy the best ice-cream in the world.'

The sight of a strange dragon selling ice-cream soon attracted the people on the beach and once they'd tasted the ice-cream they called to their friends, 'It really is the best ice-cream.'

That was the end really. Bobo went to live with Kate and her father and they all live happily to this day. Kate's father still makes perfect ice-cream, Bobo is a perfect ice-cream seller, and Kate looks after them both.

17

So if you see a dragon crying it's probably because he's longing to be able to eat ice-cream. And if you see a dragon with a blue and white top half and a dark blue bottom half selling ice-cream on the beach you'll know his name is Bobo.

David McKee

Creeping

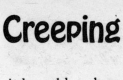

A long blue dragon
Is creeping through the village.
He's lashing his tail,
And he's tossing his head.
Run little children,
Run into your houses;
Run into your houses,
And jump into bed.

Hilde Adams

The Island of the Dragon

Once there was a dragon called Dauntless. Although he was large and powerful he was very timid. He had no desire to fight other dragons or have exciting adventures. What he enjoyed most was visiting the little town not far from the mountain cave where he lived. There he was welcomed by everyone and the children treated him like a pet, climbing on his scaley back and feeding him with buns and crisps.

The little town was by the sea and it had a long, sandy beach where the children played. Across the bay there was an island where people took their picnics. On calm, sunny days they would row out there in their boats and sit and watch the birds and the butterflies, while the children built sandcastles and played in the water.

Dauntless however was afraid of water. He didn't like the waves when they splashed all over him as they swept up the beach. The salt water got into his eyes and up his nose and made him sneeze. He could swim quite well when he tried, but he didn't even bother to go to the beach any more. He preferred to stretch himself out in the main street in the middle of the town. There he

21

could watch everyone doing their shopping, he could see the children going to and fro from school and the lorries unloading fruit and vegetables. Now this caused a great deal of trouble for everyone because he took up a lot of room and held up the traffic, but no one liked to complain as no other towns could boast they possessed a pet dragon.

Once a year, in the summer, all the school children and their teachers went to the island in the bay for a special treat. Before the fishermen went off on their day's catch, everyone piled into their boats with swimsuits and towels, buckets and spades, fishing nets and food, and they were rowed across to their special island where they could paddle, build sandcastles, collect seashells and catch little crabs in the rock-pools.

On this particular morning the sun was hot and bright and the sea calm and blue. The children waved goodbye to their parents as the fishermen loaded them into the boats and rowed them across.

They spent the morning on the beach and were just about to open their packed lunch when quite suddenly, the sky became black with thunderclouds. The waves, instead of breaking gently on the island shore, came roaring in, rushing up over the beach and into the rock-pools. The children and their teachers ran up to the top of the island where they hoped the waves would not be able to reach them. They were very, very frightened as the waves got bigger and the wind stronger and fiercer. There was no sign of the fishermen and their boats arriving to rescue them.

When the storm started everyone in the village became extremely worried. They gathered on the sea front as the waves crashed to the shore, straining their eyes to see if they could catch sight of the fishing boats returning from the island with the children. There was no sign of them! 'Oh, what shall we do,' said everyone.

Then the Lord Mayor remembered Dauntless who was lying in the middle of the town trying to keep warm and sheltering from the sea gale.

'Fetch him quickly,' said the Lord Mayor. 'He is strong and powerful. Perhaps he can swim out to the island and bring the children and their teachers safely home.'

A group of mothers and fathers hurried to explain to Dauntless that his help was needed and led him quickly to the sea. He was terrified when he saw what he had to do. When he reached the beach and saw the huge waves breaking on the shore, he thought he would die of fright. His legs trembled and he shivered and shook with cold and fright. He could hardly breathe. But everyone believed, as he stood trembling and shaking on the shore, that he was just preparing himself to plunge into the foaming water, like a plane about to take off. Dauntless realized he would have to swim to the island however scared he was. If not, he would be branded a coward for the rest of his life. He would never to able to hold up his head again.

He closed his eyes, took a deep breath and hurled himself into the foaming water, using his large dragon wings to propel himself through the waves. Soon he

realized he was swimming strongly and actually riding the billows with poise and skill. Shouts of encouragement from the shore urged him on.

He reached the island in a very short time and soon all the children and their teachers had crowded onto his back and tail and were clinging to his scales. Soon everyone was safe and sound.

All at once Dauntless realized he had been enjoying himself and his battle with the sea. He had discovered how well he could swim, plunging through the storm like a magnificent sailing ship. The children were soon landed safely.

The mothers and fathers waiting on the beach were absolutely delighted and relieved. How brave and fearless their dragon was. How proud they all were. They cheered and shouted with excitement and Dauntless was quite overcome by his own skill and courage.

The next day, when everyone had recovered from their ordeal and the fishing boats had returned safely, the village prepared to celebrate. The storm had subsided and it was bright and warm again. Tables were laid in the main street loaded with food and Dauntless was the hero of the hour. The Lord Mayor made a speech of thanks and announced that in the future the island in the bay was to be known as The Island of the Dragon.

Joan Cass

The Snitterjipe

In mellowy orchards, rich and ripe,
Is found the luminous Snitterjipe.
Bad boys who climb the bulging trees
Feel his sharp breath about their knees;
His trembling whiskers tickle so,
They squeak and squeal till they let go.
They hear his far-from-friendly bark;
They see his eyeballs in the dark
Shining and shifting in their sockets
As round and big as pears in pockets.
They feel his hot and wrinkly hide;
They see his nostrils flaming wide,
His tapering teeth, his jutting jaws,
His tongue, his tail, his twenty claws.
His hairy shadow in the moon,
It makes them sweat, it makes them swoon;
And as they climb the orchard wall,
They let their pilfered pippins fall.
The Snitterjipe suspends pursuit
And falls upon the fallen fruit;
And while they flee the monster fierce,
Apples, not boys, his talons pierce.
With thumping hearts they hear him munch –
Six apples at a time he'll crunch.
At length he falls asleep, and they
On tiptoe take their homeward way.

But long before the blackbirds pipe
To welcome day, the Snitterjipe
Has fled afar, and on the green
Only his fearsome prints are seen.

James Reeves

Albert's Christmas Party

It was Winter in Cornwall, the coldest Winter anyone could remember. Even Albert, who was nearly a hundred and forty-nine, which is young for a dragon, could only remember one other like it.

'It was when I was quite a little chap,' he told his friend Tony as the two of them struggled up the path to Albert's cave through a biting wind. They had been down to the beach, collecting driftwood for Albert's fire and were heavily laden with the pieces of smooth, bleached wood which the sea throws up on to the shore every high tide.

'I bet it wasn't as cold as this,' said Tony, rubbing his frozen nose with a red-mittened hand. 'My father says it's going to snow, and you know quite well, Albert, it hardly ever snows in Cornwall.'

'The year I'm talking about,' said Albert, 'it snowed and snowed. We youngsters loved it because we could slide and make snow-dragons and so on, but the people in your village, Tony, were in a very poor way. The road was blocked and no one could get in or out and the food began to run short.'

'Well, I hope that won't happen this year,' said Tony. 'It's nearly Christmas, and we don't want to run short of food at Christmas time. What should we do for the party?'

'Is there going to be a party?' said Albert wistfully. 'I suppose – but no, of course they won't.'

'Who won't what?' asked Tony, and Albert said shyly:

'I suppose they won't invite me?'

Tony looked at his friend's eager face and felt very uncomfortable. He knew how the people in the village felt about dragons. He had told them over and over again that Albert was a good dragon, and a vegetarian who never, never ate children or did anyone any harm, but they just didn't quite believe him.

'I'm afraid they won't, old chap,' he said reluctantly, and Albert sighed.

'Tell me about it, Tony,' he said. 'Even if I can't go I'd like to know all about it, so that I can imagine what it would be like to be there. Tell me what you do at a party.'

'Well,' said Tony, 'it's being held in my father's big barn, and the barn will be decorated with holly and ivy and mistletoe, and there'll be music and dancing and games, and half-way through we'll have a scrumptious supper, with turkey and plum pudding and mince pies and oranges and nuts and – '

'Stop!' said Albert. 'I can't take in any more. It all sounds so wonderful! Oh, Tony, how I wish I could be there!'

'I wish you could too,' said Tony. 'Poor old Albert! I'll tell you what I'll do! I'll bring you some oranges and nuts and a mince pie if I can get hold of them without being seen.'

'Oh, thank you, Tony!' said Albert gratefully. 'We could have a little party of our own the next day!'

32

'You have worried me, though,' said Tony. 'Talking about the snow. You see, the oranges and nuts and things have to come from the market town, and the fiddlers who play for the dancing come from the next village, so if the road is blocked and they can't get through we shan't have any fun at all.'

'We must hope for the best,' said Albert. 'That's all.'

But no amount of hoping did any good. Three days before Christmas the sky grew dark and the snow

began to fall, lightly at first, then thicker and thicker, until the air was full of whirling flakes and the whole countryside was covered with a deep, pure blanket of white. When Tony woke up next morning he looked out of his window and hardly knew the landscape, it was so different. He was so excited that for the moment he forgot all about the party.

'Snowball fights!' he thought joyously. 'Snowmen!

Sliding!' He hurried to put on his clothes and dashed downstairs into the kitchen where he found his mother making the porridge for breakfast.

'Oh, Mother!' he exclaimed. 'Isn't this fun?'

'Fun!' said his mother, stirring the porridge very hard. 'Fun, do you call it? And how do you think we're going to get the goodies for the Christmas party? Road be all blocked with snow and no one can get neither in nor out till it be gone. Fun, you call it!'

Tony ran to the door and looked out. He could see at once that his mother was right. There was no trace of the road which wandered over the moor to the other villages and the little market town. Tregunna Cove was quite cut off from the outside world!

'This is just like Albert said it was when he was young,' said Tony as he realized the disaster. 'He says

35

the snow blocked the road until everyone began to get short of food.'

'I don't take no account of what dragons say,' said Tony's mother. 'Pesky great things, they be! But one thing's sure: there'll be no Christmas party the day after tomorrow, for you can't give a party without goodies and music, and we can't get either if the snow don't clear.'

Tony sat down to his breakfast feeling very miserable. After breakfast he put on his boots and a warm coat and a scarf and a woolly cap and gloves and went out into the farmyard. He began to make a snowman, but it was no fun at all by himself, and the snow was so deep that none of the boys from the village could get to the farm to play with him. Finally he fetched a broom and tried to sweep a clear path from the house to the cowshed, but the broom was too big for him and the snow was too deep, and he made no headway at all.

'Bother the old snow!' exclaimed Tony crossly. 'It's going to spoil everything!'

Suddenly, from far up above him on the hillside, he heard someone calling his name.

'T–ony! T–o–ony!' shouted the voice. 'Look—at—ME!'

Tony shaded his eyes with his hand, because the sun was shining on the snow and dazzling him. He gazed up the path which led to Albert's cave and saw the most extraordinary sight. Albert, his short stumpy legs stretched straight out before and behind, was tobogganing down the steep, twisty path on his tummy, sending up a shower of powdery snow in front of him as he came!

'Oh, what fun!' thought Tony. 'I should like to do that!'

He watched Albert enviously. But just as the dragon reached the very steep turn before the farm gate,

disaster struck! He lost his balance, couldn't get round the turn, and shot right off the path and down a bank, ending up in a flurry of legs and wildly thrashing wings and tail.

'Are you hurt?' shouted Tony, and tried to run through the deep snow to help his friend, but to his relief Albert soon struggled to his feet, shook himself violently so that snow flew in all directions, and began to laugh.

'I'm all right!' he said. 'I thought, just for a moment, that I'd fractured a wing, but it's nothing, just a bruise. Oh Tony, this is tremendous fun, isn't it?'

'I don't know so much about fun,' said Tony. 'The road is blocked, and my mother says we shan't be able to have our Christmas party because no one can get out to do the shopping. I think it's mean!' And poor Tony's disappointment was so great that his eyes began to fill with tears.

'I say!' said Albert uncomfortably. 'Please don't, old chap! No really, I can't bear to see you so upset.'

'You'd be upset too,' muttered Tony, dashing his coat sleeve across his eyes to dry them, 'if you'd been going to the party and then you couldn't go because there wasn't a party after all.'

'I know exactly how you feel,' said Albert. 'It's just like I've been feeling because I wasn't invited. Awful! Oh, Tony, I do wish there was something I could do to help.'

And then a perfectly wonderful idea came into Tony's head! He thought about it and thought again, and the more he thought the better the idea seemed to be.

'Albert!' he said breathlessly. 'Can you – can you get hot whenever you want to?'

'I only get hot when I'm cross,' said Albert. 'As you very well know.'

'Well, could you please get cross?' demanded Tony. Albert stared at him in amazement.

'What have I got to get cross about?' he asked in a puzzled voice. 'I don't feel a bit cross. I'm having a lovely time tobogganing, and although I'm very sorry about your party, Tony, it only makes me sad, not cross.'

'Oh dear!' sighed Tony. 'I *do* so want you to get cross!'

'But why?' demanded the bewildered dragon.

'Well, you see,' Tony explained, 'if you got cross you'd get hot, and flames would shoot out of your nose, like they did when the Knight's horse tickled you in the ribs, and if you got *very* hot, with lots of flames you could – you could melt the snow on the road and then we could go to market and buy the goodies for our Christmas party, and the two fiddlers would be able to come and play for the dancing. Now do you understand?'

Albert gazed at Tony and his eyes were full of admiration.

'Tony, my young friend,' he said solemnly, 'I

41

always knew you were a bright boy, but I never realized before *how* bright you were! This is genius!'

'It's nothing,' said Tony modestly. 'I just thought of it. But Albert, will you do it?'

'Of course I will!' said Albert. 'Delighted! Er – there is just one small point.'

'What's that?'

'Well, somebody will have to make me cross, and at the moment I don't feel in the least cross. Quite the contrary.'

Tony thought again, harder than ever. Then suddenly he pointed a finger straight at Albert's face and said:

'Who eats children? Tell me that?'

'Not me, anyway,' said Albert. 'Don't be silly, Tony.'

'Who cheated in the fight with the Knight?' persisted Tony. 'Who can't swim as well as that lovely sea serpent? Who? Who? Who?'

'Well, really!' said Albert, and his tail began to lash gently from side to side, just like a cat's tail does if you tease it. 'Well, really!'

'Who was the old silly who built a house and burnt it down?' taunted Tony. 'Even the donkey laughed. Ha ha ha!'

'Now that's enough!' said Albert. 'I warn you, Tony, I won't stand that sort of talk!' And he began to glow with warmth, while a thin trickle of smoke came out of his nostrils and hung overhead in the frosty air.

'Silly old Albert!' jeered Tony, still pointing a finger and dancing round Albert in the snow. 'Call yourself a dragon? Who stole the feather bed?'

'I won't put up with this!' snorted Albert, and now he glowed with heat, and flames shot down his nostrils and melted the snow around him.

44

'Look, Albert, look!' yelled Tony in triumph, pointing to the melting snow. 'Now, quick, while you're still cross – go and melt the road!'

Albert stared at him, and then, suddenly he realized how clever Tony had been. He began to laugh, but Tony said quickly:

'Don't stop being cross! Silly old Albert! Who was called a dragon-napper?'

'That'll do,' said Albert quickly. 'That always makes me *furious!*' And he stamped off through the snow to the road, leaving melting snow behind him as he went.

'Mother!' shouted Tony. 'Father! Come and see what good old Albert's doing! He's clearing the road, and we shall be able to get to market after all!'

Albert pranced along the road, still red and glowing with temper. Every time he felt himself cooling down he only had to mutter 'dragon-napper' to himself, or 'sea serpent', or 'silly old donkey' and he began to boil again! All along the road people came out of their cottages to see what the noise was about, and when they saw the snow melting and leaving the road clear and dry, they cheered like anything.

'Good old Albert!' they shouted. 'Albert the People's Friend!'

Albert went all the way to the market town and then he turned and came back along the nice, dry road. He wasn't in a temper any more and he felt quite cool again, but he was very happy, because at every cottage he passed the people came out again and thanked him and praised him for being so clever. And to all of them he said modestly:

'It was nothing, no really, nothing at all. Tony thought of it. It is Tony who you ought to thank.'

But they only praised him all the more for being so modest.

When he got back to the farm, Tony and his mother and father were waiting at the gate, smiling all over their faces.

'Well done, Albert!' Tony exclaimed. 'I knew you'd do it. And, Albert, I didn't mean a word I said!'

'I'm off to market now,' said Tony's father, 'to buy all the good things for the party.' Then he hesitated and poked Tony's mother in the ribs.

'You ask him,' he muttered.

'No, you,' she said, and the farmer turned to Albert again and said:

'Will you come to our party, m'dear? You'll be right welcome, won't he, Tony?'

'You bet he will!' said Tony. 'Well, Albert, will you come?'

Albert was so overjoyed the tears came into his eyes. He put a claw on Tony's shoulder and looked into his face, but he couldn't speak, he just nodded his head.

What a party that was! Albert sat at the head of the table as the hero of the day, and Tony sat next to him. They had all the delicious things to eat that Tony had told him about, and Albert had a double helping of mince pies and oranges and nuts because he wouldn't eat turkey or ham.

After the meal there was dancing, and then right at the end, the door opened and Tony's father came in dressed as Santa Claus and gave presents to everyone. Albert's present was a pair of scarlet mittens, hastily knitted by Tony's mother, to keep his claws warm in the cold weather. He thought they were the loveliest things he had ever seen in his life. But what made him happiest, and what he thought about most when at last the party was over and he was sleepily getting ready

48

for bed in his cosy cave, was the knowledge that at long last the people of Tregunna Cove were really and truly friends with him and so he would never be a lonely dragon any more.

Rosemary Weir

So Big

The dinosaur, an ancient beast,
I'm told was very large.
His eyes were big as billiard balls,
His stomach, a garage.
He had a huge and humping back,
A neck as long as Friday.
I'm glad he lived so long ago
And didn't live in my day!

Max Fatchen

The Tale of Custard
the Dragon

Belinda lived in a little white house,
With a little black kitten and a little gray mouse
And a little yellow dog and a little red wagon,
And a realio, trulio, little pet dragon.

51

Now the name of the little black kitten was Ink,
And the little gray mouse, she called her Blink,
And the little yellow dog was sharp as Mustard,
But the dragon was a coward, and she called him
  Custard.

Custard the dragon had big sharp teeth,
And spikes on top of him and scales underneath,
Mouth like a fireplace, chimney for a nose,
And realio, trulio daggers on his toes.

Belinda was as brave as a barrel full of bears,
And Ink and Blink chased lions down the stairs,
Mustard was as brave as a tiger in a rage,
But Custard cried for a nice safe cage.

Belinda tickled him, she tickled him unmerciful,
Ink, Blink and Mustard, they rudely called him
    Percival,
They all sat laughing in the little red wagon
At the realio, trulio, cowardly dragon.

Belinda giggled till she shook the house,
And Blink said Weeck! which is giggling for a mouse,
Ink and Mustard rudely asked his age,
When Custard cried for a nice safe cage.

Suddenly, suddenly they heard a nasty sound,
And Mustard growled, and they all looked all
    around,
Meowch! cried Ink, and Ooh! cried Belinda,
For there was a pirate, climbing in the winda.

Pistol in his left hand, pistol in his right,
And he held in his teeth a cutlass bright,
His beard was black, one leg was wood;
It was clear that the pirate meant no good.

Belinda paled, and she cried Help! Help!
But Mustard fled with a terrified yelp,
Ink trickled down to the bottom of the household,
And little mouse Blink strategically mouseholed.

But up jumped Custard, snorting like an engine,
Clashed his tail like irons in a dungeon,
With a clatter and a clank and a jangling squirm
He went at the pirate like a robin at a worm.

The pirate gaped at Belinda's dragon,
And gulped some grog from his pocket flagon,
He fired two bullets, but they didn't hit,
And Custard gobbled him, every bit.

Belinda embraced him, Mustard licked him,
No one mourned for his pirate victim.
Ink and Blink in glee did gyrate
Around the dragon that ate the pyrate.

Belinda still lives in her little white house,
With her little black kitten and her little gray
   mouse,
And her little yellow dog and her little red wagon,
And her realio, trulio, little pet dragon.

Belinda is as brave as a barrelful of bears,
And Ink and Blink chase lions down the stairs,
Mustard is as brave as a tiger in a rage,
But Custard keeps crying for a nice safe cage.

Ogden Nash

Mandragora's Dragon

Once upon a time there was a castle made half of silver and half of glass. The silver half of the castle shone white as fire in the sunlight and pale as water in the moonlight, and nobody knew how high the towers were, for the clouds hid them. The other half of the castle was lovelier still, for all the glass was coloured.

Crimson and purple and rose red and blue, it sparkled like an emperor's jewel under the summer sky. But it was always cold.

Long ago the castle had been made all of silver, and then it was warm in winter when the snow drifted deep around the walls that rose up shining into a silver sky. But a dragon found it, and bit by bit he stole the walls away.

Dragons love gold and silver. Dragons collect all the gold and silver they possibly can, but however much they have, they keep on wanting more. This dragon had already collected all the gold jewellery and silver forks in the kingdom. Nobody had a necklace to wear on Sundays, and the people ate with their fingers or used wooden spoons. But the dragon still hadn't enough. He would perch on the castle towers, biting

off pieces of silver that melted like butter under his hot breath, and then he would carry them off to his cave in the hills.

When the people built the castle walls again, they had to use glass. There was no silver left. The dragon had it all.

The castle was always cold, and they had to keep fires burning night and day in the castle fireplace, which was as big as a room. Then one day in winter when the snow was eleven feet deep, they ran out of firewood. There wasn't a stick of wood left in the country. The dragon had eaten it all.

The king called his knights and nobles, and told them to drive the dragon out. They all chewed their beards and looked fierce, but none of them offered to do it. And it got colder

The king called his wise men and scholars and told them to do something about it. They all shook their heads and looked solemn, but none of them knew what to do. And it got colder.

Finally everyone went to bed, and nothing got done in the castle.

Now along with the wise men and scholars, knights, nobles, wizards, and magicians who lived in the castle, there was a cat. He was a black cat with very green eyes. And his name was Mandragora. Mandragora had such thick fur that he didn't notice the cold. So every morning and every evening he drank his dish of cream. And in between he took naps.

Then one day he found his dish of cream frozen

solid. And the next day there was no dish of cream at
all, because the cook had gone to bed.

'Well, well,' said Mandragora. 'I suppose I'll have to
catch a mouse.'

He went down in the cellar and caught a mouse, but
the mouse was as thin as a grasshopper.

'You don't look very good,' said Mandragora.

'I'm not very good,' said the Mouse, looking
nervous.

'Mice never are,' said Mandragora gloomily. 'I'd
much rather have a good dish of cream.'

'Why don't you, then?' said the Mouse.

'It's frozen,' said Mandragora. 'So I suppose you
will have to do.'

'Don't eat me,' the Mouse said. 'I'm so thin. Let me
go and I'll drive out the dragon for you.'

'You drive out the dragon?' cried Mandragora. 'You? Why, it's enough to make a cat laugh.' And he did. But he took care not to let go of the Mouse.

'I can do it, though,' said the Mouse. 'Dragons are afraid of mice.'

'Why didn't you drive him out a long time ago then?'

'Well,' said the Mouse, and he squirmed slightly, 'mice are afraid of dragons.'

'That sounds very much more likely to me,' said Mandragora.

'Let me try,' the Mouse said. 'If it doesn't work, you can always eat me afterwards.'

'And if it does work?' said Mandragora. 'What then?'

'Then you must promise never to eat mice again.'

'I wouldn't eat them at all if the cream weren't frozen,' Mandragora said, with dignity.

'Is it a bargain then?' asked the Mouse.

'It's a bargain,' agreed Mandragora.

So Mandragora and the Mouse set off for the dragon's lair. They passed a mousehole. 'Excuse me,' said the Mouse, and he popped inside. Pretty soon he came out again with four baby mice and their mother.

'My children,' he said proudly. 'ROLY, POLY, GAMMON and SPINACH. This is my wife, Mrs Mouse.'

'Pleased to meet you,' said Mrs Mouse to Mandragora.

They passed another mousehole. The Mouse went in again, and came out with seven more mice. 'My brothers,' he said.

They passed a third mousehole. He went in, and there was a lot of noise, and he came out with seven mother mice, and fourteen babies – exactly two apiece.

'My brothers' wives,' he said, 'and my nephews and nieces.'

'Ooh!' squealed all the baby mice. 'Look at the cat!'

'Behave yourselves!' said the mother mice severely.

In the next mousehole there were eleven old mice. 'My mother and father, my four aunts, and my five uncles.'

'Grandma!' squealed all the baby mice. 'Grandpa!'

They went outside into the fields. In every burrow, the Mouse had friends, or cousins-in-law, or cousins.

They climbed the hill to the dragon's lair with the Mouse and Mandragora leading, and behind them wound an endless line of mice, until the snowy white hillside was grey with them. No matter where you looked, all you could see was mice.

Way down in the cave, the dragon heard them coming. They made so much noise that he thought they were people coming to steal his treasure. He wasn't afraid of anything at all (except mice) so he came roaring out of his lair. He sailed over their heads, breathing black smoke. All the mice squeaked 'LOOK OUT!' But not one mouse ran away. Mandragora didn't run either, though he would have liked to.

Then the dragon looked down. And it wasn't people. The whole hillside was crawling with mice. He shrieked again – even louder – and shot back to his cave. All the mice ran after him.

When they got inside they saw the dragon crouched up small, right against the ceiling. He was perched on top of his highest pile of treasure. It was all the silver from the castle walls. Piled on the floor of the cave was more silver. Coins and bracelets and forks and spoons, teapots and watches and thimbles and knives – every piece of silver in the kingdom. There was gold too, and jewels. Every ring, every brooch, every baby's cup, was there in the dragon's lair. The dragon sat hunched up under the ceiling and didn't say a word.

At last, in a very trembly voice, he whispered . . . 'What do you want?'

65

Mrs Mouse began to sweep out a teapot. When she had swept it, she began to measure it for rugs. The other mice began looking for sugar bowls and cream pitchers and silver cups to live in.

'But where will I go?' the dragon whimpered. 'I'm a fire-breathing dragon. I burn things up. No one loves me.' He began to cry.

'I know a good place,' said the Mouse. 'Shall I take you there?'

'Are there any mice there?' the dragon asked between sobs.

'No,' said the Mouse. 'Not one.'

The dragon slid down from his treasure pile with a loud crash. The Mouse led him outdoors. Mandragora followed. Where the dragon breathed on the snow it turned into steam. They went downhill and across the fields till they came to the castle.

'What on earth are you bringing him here for?' asked Mandragora.

'Didn't you tell me to drive him out of the cave?'

'Yes,' said Mandragora. 'But I didn't tell you to drive him into the castle!'

'Do you want your cream to stay frozen all winter or don't you?'

'If my cream stays frozen I'll have to eat mice,' said Mandragora politely.

'All right,' said the Mouse. 'Then you let me handle this.' He led the dragon into the castle. Nobody saw them because everyone in the castle was in bed.

66

Pretty soon the Mouse came out again. He was alone. 'Look,' he said. 'Here comes the treasure.'

Mandragora looked. He saw a long line of mice winding down the hill from the dragon's lair, over the fields and into the castle yard. Every mouse had a

thimble from the castle. The sunshine made everything glitter as they moved.

'Pile it all up inside,' said the Mouse, and the long, shiny line went on into the castle.

'Well,' said the Mouse, 'good-bye now. Remember your promise.' And he disappeared after them.

Mandragora looked around. He was all alone in the snow.

'Well!' he said. 'Of all the cheats! And I still haven't had any breakfast!' He turned and went slowly indoors.

But as soon as he got inside the castle he began to notice things. First, he noticed that everyone was out of bed. The king was standing in front of the fireplace, and around him stood his wise men and scholars, secretaries, his knights and nobles, his wizards and magicians, and all the rest of the people.

They were all talking and laughing. They seemed to be very pleased. Mandragora went and looked in the fireplace.

There was the dragon, curled up inside, glowing like a hot coal and blowing smoke up the chimney.

Piled high in the four corners of the room was every bit of the treasure from the dragon's lair.

When the king and the people saw Mandragora, they all cried. 'The cat! The cat did it all! The cat has saved the castle!'

Mandragora looked modest. The king gave him several medals, and made him a duke. The people all bowed and applauded, and the cook gave him an enormous dish of cream.

The treasure from the dragon's lair went back to its proper owners, and everybody had silver forks and plenty of jewellery to wear.

The woods that the dragon had eaten grew again, and a family of bears came to live in his old cave.

The broken towers were built up again with silver. And the dragon kept the castle warm in winter when the snow drifted deep around the walls, that rose up shining into a silver sky.

Irene Elmer

Dragon Fairy

Dragon Fairy
Quite contrary
How does your green smoke flow?
Through my nose
And out it goes
With smoke rings all in a row.

Rosemary Manning

The Magician and the Dragon

Melric the magician was watching the king inspect his army. The king was angry. 'These soldiers are too fat,' he said. 'They have far too much food and too little exercise.'

It was true they weren't the smartest soldiers in the world. Their tummies bulged, their faces were smeared with chocolate cake and they had even been using their swords to make jam sandwiches.

The king had just dismissed the army when a messenger arrived, saying that a dragon had been seen in the East of the kingdom. Soon messengers were arriving from all over the country. They all brought news of dragons.

'A dragon attack!' said the king. 'This is just the challenge the army needs. Tomorrow I'll form them into teams to hunt dragons, and the most successful team will win a prize. Melric, you can stay here and keep my pet troon amused.'

Melric decided to go and have a peep at one of the dragons. He went to his room, made some signs, said some magic words, sprinkled some powder and WHOOSH! he landed beside a young and rather small dragon. The dragon was pleased to see Melric and soon they were chatting like old friends. The dragon had reached the age when dragons have to leave home to find a place of their own.

This kingdom had seemed just right, but every time he tried to make friends with the people they ran away. 'They must think I want to eat them,' he said.

'I'm sure they do,' said Melric. 'What do you eat?'

'The usual things,' sighed the dragon. 'Cornflakes, sandwiches, apples . . . anything, really. I love chocolate cake.'

'Just like the soldiers,' laughed Melric, and that reminded him of the dragon hunt.

'I can't tell the king that there's just one friendly dragon,' said Melric. 'He doesn't like me to interfere and the soldiers do need the exercise. I had better find a

74

place to hide you.' Melric magicked some sandwiches for the dragon and then went to see his sister Mertel the witch, who lived beneath a wood. Mertel said she would have loved to look after the dragon, but her place was too small. Perhaps their cousin Guz, the wizard, could help?

Guz lived on an island with lots of pets. He said he was very sorry, but all his pets had measles and it wouldn't be fair to let the dragon catch it.

Melric returned to his room to think. Tomorrow

soldiers would be searching the kingdom and nowhere would be safe for the dragon. As Melric stared thoughtfully into the fire, the smoke seemed to take the shape of a mountain, Kra's mountain, and there was Kra sitting at the top. Kra was a wise man who had helped Melric before. Now he was speaking from the fire.

'Melric,' said Kra, 'did you hear about the boy who left his toys all over his room? When his mother came in she said, "There are toys everywhere."'

'"Not everywhere," said the boy. "There are none in the toy cupboard."'

'Thank you, Kra,' said Melric. Now he knew where to hide the dragon.

The dragon was pleased to see Melric again, and to hear his plan. Melric showed the dragon the entrance to a tunnel. In the morning, when the dragon heard the soldiers leaving the castle, he was to go through the tunnel. Then Melric left the dragon for the night.

Next morning the magician and the troon waved goodbye to the king and his soldiers. The soldiers were very noisy and Melric hoped that the dragon would remember what to do when he heard them.

They set off in groups, eager to be the first to find a dragon.

Some bowmen found the first dragon. They shot it down, then found that it was a little boy's kite and they had to buy him a new one. They weren't the only keen ones. Everywhere soldiers were attacking dragons, on

carpets and paintings and even toys and fancy dress outfits.

The sign at the Red Dragon Inn had arrow holes from that day on. The innkeeper didn't mind – it made a good story to tell his customers.

A gardener suddenly had his bonfire beaten to death by some soldiers who were sure that the smoke was coming from a dragon's nose.

Everywhere it was the same story. All the soldiers thought they were risking their lives fighting fierce dragons.

All day the soldiers climbed and splashed and squelched and searched and charged and heaved and ho'd and did all sorts of other things, but not one real dragon was found. At last the king told the bugler to call them back.

When the tired soldiers had all marched home, the king said, 'Well done, men. I'm sure we have frightened away all the dragons in the kingdom.' He was wrong. When he went home to see his pet troon, there, playing with the troon was the dragon. Before the king could

say anything, Melric hastily said, 'Meet the troon's new friend. He came here to hide because it was the only place where there were no toys – I mean soldiers.'

'The troon's friend?' said the king. Now what was he going to do?

The king went up to the dragon and shook his hand. 'Why don't you live here with us, dragon?' he said. The dragon was happy to have a home at last. The king was rather pleased too – after all, who would attack an army with a dragon as a mascot? – Even if the soldiers were a bit fat!

'And what reward were you offering for finding a dragon?' Melric asked with a smile.

'Chocolate cake of course,' said the king, 'and plenty for everyone.'

David McKee